34134 00060983 1

Leabharlainn nan Eilean Siar

D0480978

BRAVE
Charlotte

J30751160

STONHER

SCHOOL
LIBRARY
STOCK

For you, who else? – H.W.

For Nina – A.S.

BLOOMSBURY
CHILDREN'S
BOOKS

First published in Great Britain in 2006 by Bloomsbury Publishing Plc,
36 Soho Square, London, W1D 3QY

First published in Germany in 2005 by Carl Hanser Verlag GmbH & Co KG
Vilshofener Strasse 10, D-81679, Munich, Germany

This paperback edition first published in 2007 by Bloomsbury Publishing Plc

Original Title: Das Schaf Charlotte
Copyright © Carl Hanser Verlag München Wien 2005

All rights reserved
No part of this publication may be reproduced or
transmitted by any means, electronic, mechanical, photocopying
or otherwise, without the prior permission of the publisher

A CIP catalogue record of this book is available from the British Library

ISBN 0 7475 8102 9
ISBN-13 9780747581024

Printed in China by South China Printing Co.

10 9 8 7 6 5 4 3 2 1

All papers used by Bloomsbury Publishing are natural, recyclable products
made from wood grown in well-managed forests. The manufacturing processes
·conform to the environmental regulations of the country of origin.

BRAVE
Charlotte

by Anu Stohner

illustrated by Henrike Wilson

BLOOMSBURY
CHILDREN'S
BOOKS

WESTERN ISLES LIBRARIES	
J30751160	
Bertrams	28.05.07
	£5.99

Nobody knew why Charlotte was different from all the other sheep. But she had been like it right from the start. When all the other lambs just stood shyly by their mothers …

... Charlotte was bounding around, ready for an adventure.

Jack, the old sheepdog, tried to keep Charlotte in line, but she wasn't scared of him.

One day Charlotte went missing and the shepherd found her up a tree. Jack tried to chase her down but Charlotte wanted to stay up there a little longer, and only moved when she was ready.

"*Tut, tut, tut,*" said the old sheep, shaking their heads disapprovingly. "Where is this all going to end?"

But that was just the beginning. Another time, Charlotte jumped over the side of a riverbank and went for a swim in the fast-running stream.

"*Tut, tut, tut,*" said the older sheep,
shaking their heads.
"*Tut, tut, tut.*"

Before long, Charlotte was up to more mischief. She had climbed to the very top of the highest peak – something no other sheep had ever done before!

"Oh, oh, oh!" groaned the other sheep. They were hardly able to watch because it made them feel dizzy.

When they found Charlotte on the side of a dangerously busy road, staring at the oncoming traffic, all the sheep wanted to know what she was doing. But Charlotte didn't want to tell them.

"Oh my goodness!" exclaimed the old sheep. "What is she up to?"

What would they say if they knew that at night Charlotte secretly roamed through the countryside?

When all the others were
sleeping, she would quietly
slip away to her special
place and gaze at the
moon. Even Jack didn't
notice anything out of the
ordinary. But he didn't
have very good ears
these days.

Then, in autumn, as the days were getting
shorter and the nights darker, something
terrible happened. The shepherd fell over and
broke his leg. Jack barked and circled around
him but sadly that didn't help one bit, and so
the shepherd lay in the grass, not knowing
what to do.

"Oh dear, oh dear, oh dear," said the older
sheep. "Somebody must go to the farmer's
house in the valley and get help."

"Jack should go. He is the only one who knows the way."
"But it is too far. He hardly even manages with the herd these days."
"Yes, that's true," said the others, shaking their heads in despair.

Then Charlotte said, "I'll do it. I'll go."
"Charlotte?" muttered the older sheep.
"The little rascal?"
"Out of the question!"
"A sheep has never gone to the valley alone."
"Absolutely not!"

The older sheep were beside themselves with worry, but Charlotte could no longer hear them. She had already reached the big oak tree, and was trying to find the right way to the valley.

She bounded over fields,

through the fast-running stream,

and over the mountain tops,

until it got dark.

When Charlotte reached the busy road, it was the middle of the night.
She stood at the side of the road and watched the oncoming traffic.
The lights of the cars shone. So did Charlotte's eyes.

A truck driver noticed Charlotte's shining eyes and stopped in the road.
"Going to the valley?" he asked kindly.
Charlotte nodded.

It was so nice to roar through the night in the truck
that Charlotte was almost sorry to have to get out.

"Take care," said the friendly truck driver.
"You too!" thought Charlotte.

The farmer was asleep when Charlotte tapped on the
windowpane with her nose.
"A sheep," said the farmer's wife, who woke up first.
"It's Charlotte," said the farmer, "and she is all
alone. Something must be up."

Charlotte and the farmer drove on the tractor to find the other sheep. When they arrived, the poor shepherd was still lying in the grass. The farmer took him to the hospital without delay.

The shepherd had his leg in plaster for three weeks, and then he was able to go back to the sheep. "He's not a youngster any more," said the older sheep. "Just like Jack." "*Tut, tut, tut.*" "What will happen to us?" they wondered.

"As long as Charlotte is here to watch over us, we should be OK."
"That's very true."
And so they continued to chatter and shake their heads.
And Charlotte?

Charlotte was off exploring with Jack!